The
Billionaire and
the Monk

The Billionaire and the Monk

AN INSPIRATIONAL STORY
ABOUT FINDING
EXTRAORDINARY HAPPINESS

Vibhor K. Singh

balance

NEW YORK BOSTON

Copyright © 2022 by Vibhor K. Singh

Cover design by Jarrod Taylor. Cover illustration by Patrick Morgan. Cover copyright © 2022 by Hachette Book Group, Inc.

Balance
Hachette Book Group
1290 Avenue of the Americas, New York, NY 10104
grandcentralpublishing.com
twitter.com/grandcentralpub

Originally published in India by Notion Press Publishing
First U.S. Edition: May 2022

Balance is an imprint of Grand Central Publishing. The Balance name and logo is a trademark of Hachette Book Group, Inc.

The publisher is not responsible for websites (or their content) that are not owned by the publisher.

The Hachette Speakers Bureau provides a wide range of authors for speaking events. To find out more, go to www.hachettespeakersbureau.com or call (866) 376-6591.

LCCN: 2021950104

ISBNs: 978-1-5387-0941-2 (paper over board), 978-1-5387-2229-9 (ebook)

Printed in the United States of America

LSC-C

Printing 1, 2022

For my father,
the late Kunwar Onkar Singh (1950–2013),
who taught me to maintain a sense of humor
even in the most difficult of times.
Life has been beautiful because of this teaching.

Contents

Prologue   1

1. The Road to Shangri-La   5

2. It Starts with the Mind   13

3. Simplicity of Happiness   25

4. The Don't Blame Game   31

5. Budge the Grudge   39

6. Healthy Body, Happy Body   47

7. Buying Happiness   55

8. Homecoming: The Monk's Story   67

9. Choosing the Path: The Billionaire's Story   73

10. Farewell   79

Epilogue   83

Knowledge Points   85

Letter from the Author   89

Acknowledgments   93

The Billionaire and the Monk

"The best time to plant a tree was 20 years ago.
The second-best time is now."

—ANCIENT CHINESE PROVERB

PROLOGUE

"Success is not the key to happiness. Happiness is the
key to success. If you love what you are doing, you will
be successful."

—ALBERT SCHWEITZER

Sitting in the presidential suite facing Central Park in New
York, the Billionaire was preparing for the interview. He
was among the 2,153 people in the world called *Dollar Bil-
lionaires*, a sincere acknowledgment of human achievement
and perseverance. He had not inherited the title, and that
had made him more special in the eyes of the world. In
a single lifetime, he had achieved wealth that some countries took generations to accumulate. He was proud of his
achievements.

The interview was along expected lines. The public
relations agency he had hired was the best in the world, and

it had left no stone unturned to project him as a humble yet ambitious man—an ordinary man with big dreams. Some called him the Deal Bull. Blessed with a sharp mind that effortlessly understood the stock market and persevering entrepreneurial deal-making acumen, he had pioneered a business style that was unmatched and unbeatable.

However, the last question by the interview host had unsettled him. Though he had answered the question confidently, in his signature style, something had pricked him within. The question was not part of the script that had been handed to him earlier. Probably, the question was considered a mere formality or an insignificant last comment. However, for him, this last question had made every other aspect of the evening, in fact his entire life, irrelevant.

"Are you happy?" the girl had asked.

As the day drew to an end, the Monk settled in his dining seat, lost in thought as he stared at the steam from his momo soup bowl rise, dance in curls, and vanish into the air. *Non-permanency is also the nature of human existence. We are born of the Supreme Soul and have only some time to make our presence felt in the world before we vanish again into the Supreme Soul.*

Even though it had been 30 years since he had walked out of the monastic order and surrendered his monkhood, he was a highly respected and knowledgeable man. People still honored him with the title of Monk.

After dinner, the Monk felt the urge to go and meet his guruji—the Chief Lama—to clear his mind. Something was troubling him. It was a bright moonlit night, and the golden roof of the monastery was reflecting silver. It only proved to him that perspective was more important than substance. A gentle breeze brought with it the chill of the mountains. As he walked alone through the stone-cobbled streets of the sleepy old town, he imagined that it was probably on a night like this a prince had left behind all his material possessions, earthly relations, and a magnificent palace to walk the path of knowledge. The prince never returned; instead, the Great Buddha was born.

It was probably a sin to compare himself with the Buddha, but his heart had been agitated for the past few weeks and he was unable to control his emotions of late. The Chief Lama had once explained that all journeys of self-discovery and inner peace start by asking the right questions. Today was probably that day in his life where more than answers he needed the right question.

As he turned into the street opposite the Chief Lama's house, he came face to face with graffiti on the wall. He read it and froze. Was it his heart that was playing a trick, or was it divine intervention? The Monk turned back and returned to his room without meeting the Chief Lama.

He had found his question. Written on the wall were three words:

Are you happy?

CHAPTER 1

THE ROAD TO SHANGRI-LA

"You can't depend on your eyes when your
imagination is out of focus."

—MARK TWAIN

"If happiness is a journey, minimalism is the first step," the Monk said to the Billionaire. Even though the statement had been made without any context, the Billionaire shut his eyes in agreement.

His mind went back to when they had first decided to partner together. The first meeting in the hotel in Kathmandu had done the trick for both of them. The Billionaire had seen an opportunity to do something genuinely different from his regular deals—a hotel in Shangri-La was the ultimate trophy asset to have. The Monk had seen the partnership as a bridge to reconnect with the materialist world. Both knew the mutual benefit of the collaboration and had respected it. And today, two years later, the Billionaire knew he had made a profitable decision. Even though this was his first visit to the hotel, his team and the Monk had executed a capital-efficient project and the Billionaire was happy with the accolades that the hotel was receiving in the travel industry.

He'd initially worried that having a Buddhist monk as a partner was going to be difficult. *What did a monk know about business?* However, now, holding the balance sheet of the hotel project, the Billionaire was pleased to have been proved wrong.

Retracing his thoughts back to the Monk's statement, the Billionaire reflected that as a child, the first thought that had been implanted in the Billionaire's mind was to associate happiness with hoarding and accumulating material goods. Showcasing abundance was regarded as the key to happiness in his society. Shunning abundance was viewed as a failure. However, somewhere in his heart, he needed to discover how this habit of hoarding and accumulation was nothing but clutter and one of the hindrances in pursuing happiness in his life. *Maybe the Monk could help?*

"Minimalism is not the absence of ambition. It is not sainthood. It is a life choice in which you decide to live with minimum possessions but with maximum focus. The idea is that through physical unclutter, you also unclutter your mental cupboards, which remain loaded with unnecessary and meaningless objects and emotions," the Monk said as if he had read the Billionaire's mind.

"I guess having less stuff to carry makes it easier to take on the road of life," responded the Billionaire sarcastically.

The drive through the rugged yet peaceful Tibetan landscape was beginning to calm the Billionaire's nerves. It had been a hectic 24 hours with both jet-lagged intercontinental travel and some bad news accompanying him on this trip. The telecom deal in Kazakhstan was not shaping up as required. The bureaucracy was stalling the final sign-off on the license. Some palms had to be greased, but the Billionaire had refused to oblige.

Getting his thoughts back to the present, the Billionaire knew the meaning of modern minimalism; after all, it was the latest fad globally. The billionaire Nicolas Berggruen was a vocal follower of modern minimalism. On the face of it, minimalism was a lifestyle that advocated having few physical possessions. It merely encouraged you to identify what was essential for you to survive and throw away everything else. Every material possession had to justify its existence in your daily life. The only problem was that he thought of minimalism as a hippie lifestyle.

"Much easier," smiled the Monk, bringing the Billionaire back into the discussion. "But you see, once you decide to go minimalistic in your life, you in effect start dropping *all* unnecessary pieces of baggage; you begin to see the real goals and experience the energy to achieve them effectively. It is not an excuse to run away from your responsibilities. It is not an ambition-free life. It is certainly not an excuse for being lazy! You are merely deciding to focus on a few but essential things and shun distractions. By focusing your energy on few but essential things, you can cut out distractions and attain happiness in a far more efficient manner."

To think of it, the Monk was correct, the Billionaire mused. *Some of the most significant achievers of the present times, like Jeff Bezos, the richest man on the planet, Bill Gates, Warren Buffett, and the prodigy Mark Zuckerberg, are famous for their ability to live a simple, focused life. They even attribute their success to the fact that they can cut out distractions and focus only on essential aspects; this, in effect, helps them concentrate on the big picture.*

"So, minimalism supports your ambition?" questioned the Billionaire in a curious tone. The sky was beginning to turn gray with threatening clouds. It seldom rained in this part of the world, but the dance of the clouds was always theatrical.

"Yes, as we move from the physical aspect of minimalism

to the mental acceptance of minimalism, it gives us the freedom to pursue what is essential. The truth is that the only reason we continue to live with a lot of clutter is that we are afraid to let go. We think we may need what is useless today, someday. Our fear and insecurity are the most significant reasons we are reluctant to embrace minimalism. We feel society will look down on us, our social standing will get dented, and our ambition and dreams will die if we embrace minimalism." The last sentences of the Monk were meant to help the Billionaire make the right choice. The Billionaire understood, and it brought a faint smile.

Surprisingly, a drizzle had started by now. The Monk wound down the car windows, and the earthy fragrance of rain hitting parched soil filled the car. It was intoxicating. "Funny, we may differentiate among ourselves based on countries and race, but everywhere, petrichor smells just the same," the Billionaire mumbled to himself.

The Monk heard it. "Yes, humans differentiate; nature doesn't."

"So, tell me, how would you want me to practice minimalism without having to give up my bank balance?" asked the Billionaire. Philanthropy was not his forte, and he had no intention of donating his hard-earned fortune to charity.

"Minimalism is not about giving up your bank balance, partner; it can add to it!" said the Monk with a wink and smile. "Let me run you through the main components of minimalism as I understand them: I believe that the road to happiness starts with shedding some luggage. However, unlike the Great Buddha, we don't always have to renounce the world. This is where my guruji at the monastery and I often quarrel. I am against total renunciation and want to find happiness in the world, not away from the world. I see minimalism as the first step to my goal of happiness." The Monk was serious now. "I have been studying and trying to find the answers to happiness via minimalism. I may have reached somewhere, but I am not sure. Maybe, we can bring our thoughts together? Why don't you take out the pocket diary from the glove box; I have been scribbling my thoughts on it," the Monk said, pointing toward the glove box.

The Billionaire found the diary and opened it. On the first page was the photo of the Dalai Lama. Since it is forbidden to carry the picture, most Tibetans hide the image of His Holiness among their daily use items. On the third page was scribbled the following:

1. Minimalism is both for physical and emotional baggage.
2. Physical minimalism is the first step toward mental and emotional happiness.

3. Humans are resourceful and can innovate to live without and within.
4. Minimalism boosts ambition by helping us focus.
5. The greatest gift of minimalism is the free time that gets generated and can be used to pursue what is meaningful.
6. Minimalism is gentle on the planet. Practicing minimalism is our way of contributing.
7. Don't carry the load of the world on your shoulders.

The Billionaire reread the page and, after giving it a thought, added the following:

8. Money saved is money earned.
9. Remember, we are not becoming saints by pursuing minimalism; we are only becoming selective in our pursuits and goals.
10. Don't participate in consumerism and bankrupt your wallet and happiness.

The Billionaire could not stop his smile as he noticed that he had written the words with his latest Montblanc pen; irony just died.

"Let's do one thing. I am here for three weeks. Since I will not be submerged with work here, I think I will have time to think about matters beyond work. Let's decide to make a list of things that bring happiness to our lives and share those between ourselves on the last day of this trip. What say you?" the Billionaire asked excitedly.

"This sounds brilliant; I will finally be able to share my views on happiness and learn about happiness from someone who is a hard-core capitalist." Both burst into laughter.

CHAPTER 2

IT STARTS WITH THE MIND

"To enjoy good health, to bring true happiness to one's
family, to bring peace to all, one must first discipline
and control one's mind. If a man can control his mind,
he can find the way to enlightenment, and all wisdom
and virtue will naturally come to him."

—THE BUDDHA

The Government of China, in 2001, had renamed the
sleepy village of Zhongdian to the mythical Shangri-La
of *Lost Horizon* fame. It was a brilliant marketing plan to
build a tourism destination from scratch and let the Western world experience the serenity and tranquility of Tibet.
Zhongdian was chosen because it had all the three critical
elements mentioned in the story—a breathtaking beautiful

Tibetan landscape, relics of a World War II warplane that had been discovered near the village border, and the presence of the enchanting Songtsen Ling Monastery. To think of it, maybe Zhongdian was the Shangri-La that James Hilton imagined.

The Billionaire had read about the development at Shangri-La and grabbed the first opportunity to start a joint venture with the Monk. The latter had been highly recommended for his resourcefulness by the Billionaire's contacts in the Government of China. It was a small hotel, but the idea of beating all his peers to the destination was a significant boost to the Billionaire's ego.

The Billionaire loved his morning chai. Sweet masala chai was his preferred drink. *Drinkers of coffee are always the "pretenders" and not to be trusted. Chai drinkers, on the other hand, are the ones who are grounded and can be trusted.*

This morning was different. Now that he had started to look at the world through the lens of minimalism, the beauty in the lightness of life was evident to him.

He believed that the human mind is the most powerful tool that is within our control. The Billionaire knew that scientifically speaking, the brain controls our emotional well-being through the release of neurotransmitters like dopamine and serotonin, which are responsible for the "happiness" emotion that we experience. Furthermore, all feelings, like fear, anxiety, pain, and depression, are born in the mind and can be killed in the mind itself. The power to think, imagine, decide, and act all lies within the gambit of the mind. Given this essential physiological role, our happiness quotient is related to our state of mind. But all knowledge is not easy to follow.

After yesterday's discussion, he saw the importance of uncluttering his mental storage and replacing the clutter with a happiness resort to attain everlasting joy and happiness—a resort as serene as the one he had built in Shangri-La.

"Did you sleep well?" The Monk's question startled the Billionaire from his thoughts. "Hope the room was warm?"

"Yes, all good; the Swiss did a fantastic job with the floor heating. I will email my office this afternoon to write an official letter of appreciation to their CEO. But I did end up thinking about our discussion on minimalism yesterday. Minimalism is fine, but I think more variables are needed to make you happy in life. After all, if happiness lies only in minimalism, the world would have come to a standstill. No material progress for humankind would ever have taken shape. Am I making sense?"

The Monk did not expect the first thoughts of the day to be minimalism on a billionaire's mind. But years of dealing with inquisitive minds made him understand the thoughts racing in the Billionaire's mind. "I agree. Happiness is more than just minimalism. Just last week, I met a fascinating elderly American couple who shared some very profound insights on their learnings in life. Let's discuss this over breakfast, shall we?"

Both the Billionaire and the Monk liked to have a substantial breakfast. Since both of them had spent their early years struggling, they regarded lunch as a luxury. So, breakfast was always a well-consumed meal.

"Mr. and Mrs. Fanning are first-generation entrepreneurs, like you, and own some oil rigs in Texas. They are probably in their early 70s, and they were here to celebrate their 40th anniversary. What attracted me toward them was the aura of happiness around them. Also, the discipline they followed even at this age is remarkable. They seemed to have all their activities planned like clockwork, be it entertainment or meals. They enjoyed but never indulged, if I may say so.

"So, I asked Mr. Fanning how he managed to keep up with this discipline and still be happy.

" *'Happiness begins with defining your goals and pacing your life accordingly,'* he remarked.

" *'Define your goals.* An essential step toward happiness is to bring focus to your thoughts. Remember, where focus goes, energy flows. Therefore, it is imperative to know where you are going before you start walking on the road to happiness. Remove all confusion and replace it with well-defined goals.'

"He explained to me the 'weekend goal setting' game that he loves to share with people. It goes something like this.

1. Friday—Just before sleeping, think, in silence, and write down the 20 most important goals you want to achieve. Categorize them however you like, materialist, professional, social, physical, and emotional goals if you wish. You must write these goals with honesty and sincerity. Put this piece of paper under your pillow and let the goals be the last thought to occupy your mind before you fall asleep.

2. Saturday—When you wake up, delete five of the least essential goals from the list. The elimination does not have to be category wise. The five least important goals across the list get deleted. During the day, think about the goals and also ponder if you need to add something. Later on at night, when you are at peace with yourself, delete another five. If you have

added something to the list, delete the corresponding number so that only ten goals are left. Once again, sleep with the goals under your pillow.

3. Sunday—When you wake up, delete another five. Now you are left with only five goals. These five goals are the purpose of your life. Live with them and live for them. Identify the skills, people, and tools required to achieve them.

4. Before going to bed on Sunday, write down the skills, people, and tools that you have identified against each goal. Put this final list of your goals and the pathway toward them under your pillow and sleep with the satisfaction that you have begun the mental journey to attaining happiness.

5. Every night before sleeping, go over this list. These goals and the pathway should be your last thoughts before sleeping. Gradually, the mind will filter out all other ideas, and your focus on these goals will be visible in all your actions.

"Once you begin to do this, you move to the next step, which is living by a *to-do list*." The Monk paused to take a sip of his chai.

"I also like to live by a to-do list," interrupted the Billionaire. The enthusiasm to share his thoughts was childlike.

"The productive benefit of making a to-do list cannot be overemphasized. It is an essential tool that helps us remove the mundane and focus on the necessary. A to-do list is best prepared in the morning so that you can plan your day around it. In the morning, the mind is calm and in a better state to process a 360-degree aspect of the day ahead.

"Overloading the list will discourage you from pursuing it. So, it is best to keep the list simple, numbered, and precise so that it supports the mind and does not overwhelm it. At night, check the to-do list and tick the completed tasks. Hopefully, you would have been able to close all jobs, but if something is incomplete, don't worry. Complete it the next day.

"The satisfaction of ticking the closed tasks is confidence-boosting, encouraging, and energizing for future missions. It will help you focus and achieve more." The Billionaire finished the sentence with a glow of achievement. He was hoping to get an appreciation star from his teacher!

Another great mind now validated Mr. Fanning's secret.

After breakfast, both the partners visited the governor of the province. The governor was the face of the Government of China and was always delighted to meet investors and inquire about their state of affairs. Remaining in touch helped provide comfort to the investors and also possibly helped in attracting more investments into the region. The Government of China valued investors like no other country, and this was partly responsible for the growth trajectory the country had witnessed over the past decades.

The Billionaire strongly believed that China was a capitalist society in socialist clothing, whereas India was a socialist society in capitalist clothing.

The governor was a cute-looking 55-year-old, if that is something that can be said. His eyes smiled more than his lips. Even though the Billionaire did not understand the language, the genuine show of happiness and concern displayed by the governor was enough to make the Billionaire feel welcomed and loved by this country. Happiness was contagious, he guessed.

On their way back to the resort, the Monk took the Billionaire to meet the Chief Lama. True to the philosophy of enlightenment, the Lama's room was bare and adorned with only the essentials. As luck would have it, the Lama had just finished his meditation, and there was a divine glow of bliss on his face. The Monk had often talked about the Billionaire, and the Lama was happy to finally meet the visionary man, who was able to see both the financial potential and the positive social impact of investing in a project like this.

The Lama, like many of his people, had spent some time in India in his childhood. He had the highest respect for Indians because of the support they had provided His Holiness the Dalai Lama. He insisted on hosting the Billionaire for a simple meal of rice and lentils. The Lama jokingly inquired if the Billionaire had brought any pickles from India. Since time immemorial, Indians had traveled globally as merchants and businessmen and not as invaders. They had carried with them their culture, food, and wisdom. From his days in Dharamshala, the Lama loved mango pickle. *Simple joys are often the most fulfilling.*

As they waited for lunch, presiding over the traditional tea ceremony, the discussion found its way to meditation.

"As per ancient wisdom and scriptures, meditation, in different forms and formats, has been practiced to calm the mind and focus energy," the Lama explained. "Meditation can mean different things to different people. Several schools of thought and techniques exist, and each has its own merits and demerits. However, the goal of all meditation techniques is the same—*bring harmony to the mind, the body, and soul.* So, in my view, anything that helps you attain harmony is meditation. I am not a stickler for the regular yogic meditations."

Harmony is a passive vocabulary word and rarely used as part of one's active vocabulary. When used at the correct time, it has a pleasant ring to it. The Billionaire was pleased to hear it in this ambiance and company.

"For some people, yoga is meditation, whereas for some, even a walk in the garden is meditation. For some, chanting is meditation, whereas for some, listening to Kishore Kumar's melodies is also meditation." The last words were aimed at the Monk, who loved his Bollywood tunes. "The truth is, listening to your thoughts in silence while drinking a cup of chai is also meditation. In effect, don't go by any laid-down or preconceived definitions of meditation; instead, anything that helps you make that one microsecond connection with your soul is meditation. Pursue it. It is the single most potent source of all energy and happiness in your life. Don't bother how anyone else wants you to meditate; you alone know what works for you. Stick to it." The Lama smiled and pointed at the steaming bowl of rice and dal that had been placed before each of them.

The Lama's explanation of meditation made sense to the Billionaire. The Billionaire had never been able to sit in an "ideal" position and meditate. No matter what he tried, his hyperactive mind would always wander off. But if the definition just given by the Lama was right, he did meditate every day when he had his morning cup of tea! His chai time was his me time; it was his meditation.

How did the Lama know? Coincidence or divine guidance? The Billionaire knew that the path to happiness had started to reveal itself.

CHAPTER 3

SIMPLICITY OF HAPPINESS

"Beauty is the promise of happiness."

—STENDHAL

"What is that presentation that is keeping you occupied in the morning?" inquired the Monk, hoping not to sound too prying.

"It's a study on the future of the telecommunication industry and how people are consuming data globally," replied the Billionaire in a matter-of-fact manner, while continuing to stare at his iPad.

"Is it true that the human race is standing at an inflection point that has been stimulated by the introduction of virtual life and digital existence? Is it the new cocaine?" asked the Monk, fully knowing that *now* he was disturbing the Billionaire. But asking was always the Monk's favorite hobby. After all, as a monk, he had learned that asking was the first step to receiving!

The Billionaire put down the iPad on the table and replied after a pause, "It is without a doubt that exposure to the smartphone and the virtual world overall is both a milestone and a curse in the human evolution chain. It will have long-lasting implications for the human race, something that cannot be visualized today even by the finest minds of our generation. I feel it is essential for us to embrace technology but with precautions. After all, we have to understand that technology in our lives today should be a servant and not a master. It is a tool that can add immense value to our daily lives, but the moment technology begins to control us, it calls for a review of our relationship with technology.

"It is common knowledge that screen time, primarily via a personal device like the smartphone, is altering not only our social interaction habits but also the power of the mind. We, as a society, are moving toward comfort from a virtual existence as it requires minimum physical exertions. Moreover, various studies are increasingly pointing toward the possibility that this digital overload may be a primary source of problems like anxiety, distraction, depression, and unhappiness.

"The urge to check your phone regularly, the sense of rejection which gets implanted when your social post does not elicit a response, or the very depressing task of comparing your real life with the virtual life of another is leading to severe mental health issues and causing widespread unhappiness. It is, therefore, becoming essential to learn how to *switch-off*! Yes, switching off your mobile is now a critical daily task just like brushing your teeth. Keeping your phone beside your bed at night is more toxic to your happiness than you can think. It may be a harmless habit, but the damage it does on the unconscious mind is manifold. This urge to always remain connected 24/7 and participate in the 'Age of Attention' is draining the simple joys of our lives."

Age of Attention? The Monk had heard about the Stone Age, the Iron Age, the Industrial Age, and, in a sense, even the capitalist age, but he was hearing the term Age of Attention for the first time. However, the context in which it was spoken was easily understood by him.

"However, practicing screen distancing is more difficult than it sounds," interrupted the Monk, jokingly pointing at the Billionaire's iPad.

"This only proves my point," chuckled the Billionaire. "The time that people spend on social media, watching web series, and other mindless consumption of digital content, without any purpose or aim, is turning us into zombies. It is making people lose focus on daily activities and hampering productivity at work. We hear about tragedies that happen when people risk their lives to record a video or take a selfie. I guess you can never underestimate the stupidity of human obsessions. It may be good for my business, but I make sure that for my kids, in my house, the consumption of online content is regulated and a strict time limit is imposed on screen exposure. Since I know the side effects, I make sure it does not become a nuisance."

As an afterthought, the Billionaire added, "Hypocrisy is common in capitalism."

The Billionaire resumed his work on the iPad. The Monk wandered away to see why the new tourists were singing their football team anthem in the reception area. Probably, their football team had won. *There was always something new to learn in the hotel industry.* He smiled.

The Billionaire needed a break and decided to go and take a quick nap. The slow pace of life at Shangri-La was helping him catch up on decades of lost sleep!

In the afternoon, the partners were supposed to drive to the Pudacuo National Forest Park, to plan how trips to the park could get added to the tour itinerary for hotel guests.

❀ ❀ ❀

The beauty of the park was mesmerizing. The rolling meadows, the blue mountains, and the shimmering lakes made a picture-perfect setting. Ancient pine and cypress trees formed the backdrop to the crystal-clear waters. The hills were gentle and alive. Adding to the beauty of the landscape was the musical orchestra of the various black-necked cranes that had blessed this land by making it their home. This experience at this moment was, without doubt, unadulterated happiness.

Just then, the Billionaire's thoughts drifted toward the concrete jungle he called home—Mumbai.

He mused over how most humans, the residents of the concrete jungle kingdom, live. *Some of us are in love with the city skylines, some of us find music in the city commotion, and for some of us, the gastronomic delights of city life are irresistible. The window shopping, the club-hopping, and the traffic choir are all part and parcel of our existence. Love it or hate it; it is there. However, in all this, we miss the purity of nature, as I am experiencing. This is probably why some people stick "mountains are calling" bumper stickers to cars.*

His thoughts continued to drift.

Nature is the ultimate healer. It is a limitless source of happiness, and we concrete jungle residents have to bring that happiness into our daily lives. Breathing in nature and not cosmetic representations should be incorporated in our lifestyle through design and arrangements. Maybe having potted plants, incorporating airy architectural designs, adopting pets, making time for lazy sunrise and sunset gazing, going on nature walks and picnics, and listening to music that represents the sounds of nature can help bring nature and its positivity into our lives. Embracing nature, even through the smallest acts, can help us remove the mundane and pursue the meaningful. Maybe my wife's theory that a walk in the park can calm your nerves and save you a dozen trips to the doctor is actually correct. A single stoke of nature can paint our daily lives with colors of happiness. Amen.

As his thoughts manifested, he realized the simplicity of these ideas was empowering.

Not forgetting that escapism via travel and tourism is a billion-dollar industry globally, the Billionaire and the Monk raised a toast to their tourism investments!

The drive back to the resort was in silence. Happiness and beauty are sometimes best enjoyed in lonely silence.

CHAPTER 4

THE DON'T BLAME GAME

"Most folks are as happy as they
make up their minds to be."
—ABRAHAM LINCOLN

The Monk was agitated, in fact quite "unmonkly," in the
morning. Some guests had vanished with valuable hotel
belongings when they had checked out in the wee hours.
Bloody thieves! It was a mistake to have obliged his travel
agent friend who had booked the group. The Monk had
wanted to say no, but fear of losing social approval had
restrained him, and now he was paying the price. The
housekeeping manager was flushing red as the Monk steam-
rolled him with the choicest abuses.

The Billionaire had just finished his morning cup of chai

and was carefully watching his partner blame and disrespect the hotel staff. He understood the frustration, but seeing an agitated monk was like witnessing an oxymoron come to life. The Billionaire thought that for once, it was his turn to teach his partner a few lessons on happiness, which the Billionaire had deciphered from the mysteries of life.

"You know *being grateful and not blaming* are essential to attain happiness in life," the Billionaire remarked, coming straight to the topic as the partners sat down for their breakfast. Though the Monk had calmed down by now, the signs of the morning war cries were still evident on his face.

"Trust me when I say this, but when we forget these two doctrines, life suddenly starts taking a turn for the worse. Most people will agree that we spend a lot of time thinking about all the good things that could have happened to our lives but did not, because of someone or something. It could be a colleague's actions, a childhood event, a career choice we made, or an investment decision we did not make. The fact remains: The past cannot be undone. No amount of vengeance, praying, remorse, or remedial action can fix the past; what can be adjusted are the present-day consequences of the past.

"Moreover, it is liberating to know that you and only

you alone have control over your own life. This understanding is essential to be happy. The moment you start blaming others for the state of affairs in your life, you are ceding control and surrendering your right to happiness. Once you take responsibility for your actions, even if they turn out to be disastrous, they provide you with a learning opportunity. However, when you start playing the blame game, your mind is more concerned about putting together a 'blame list' and it stops processing the lessons that could have been learned from the disaster.

"*It is, therefore, essential to stop blaming.*

"It is often said, and I fully agree, that if all of us were to put our troubles on the table and compare them with those of each other, most of us would be happy to walk away with our existing problems itself! Yes, a strange but true observation.

"Everyone is fighting his own battle, which is unknown to others, and everyone is suitably equipped to fight that battle. In other words, your troubles are just the right troubles for you. It is, therefore, essential to *be grateful for what you have* and stop crying about *what you could have had*. What you have or don't have has been designed as per your needs, and this generosity of karma should be valued and appreciated. It is essential to learn to be grateful to be happy."

The Monk listened attentively, his features relaxing as he absorbed what the Billionaire was saying.

"But remember," continued the Billionaire, "being grateful does not mean that you live in a status quo without aspirations; it does not mean that you give up trying to progress or move ahead in life. It only means that you cherish the present and build the future on the present." The Billionaire concluded his explanation, and the monologue made the Monk realize his mistake. The habit of blaming could make one lame in the journey to happiness. He was also happy to see his partner in a new light. Only a sensitive human being knew the importance of being grateful.

The Monk apologized to the housekeeping manager and with a wink and smile thanked his partner for showing him the right path. After all, the Monk had lots to be grateful for in his life.

As the day progressed, the Monk continued to think of the morning's event. He was anxious to learn why the incident had made him so furious. Customers vanishing with hotel stuff was a regular occurrence. So, what drove him to an extreme reaction this time around? He needed to understand the real reason behind his rage. Maybe, a quick chat with his guruji would help him.

The Lama listened to the Monk's narrative of the morning's events. The Monk's innocence of repeating the abuses he hurled at the housekeeping staff verbatim made the Lama smile. Some of the verbal abuses reminded him of the good old days in Dharamshala, where tourists from Delhi would use abuses as punctuation marks, but all in good humor. By the time the Monk finished narrating the event, the Lama had understood the cause of the Monk's agitation.

"Now that you have decided to return to the commercial world," the Lama spoke in a soft but firm voice, "you need to understand the one most important trait for success and happiness in life. You need to learn to say NO." The Lama paused to look at the bird that had just sat on the window. *Had it also come to hear him speak?*

"A lot of unhappiness in our life is created because we have not been taught to say NO. Most of us are afraid to say NO to people, situations, and relationships because we fear social boycott, economic deprivation, or are simply scared of change.

"We are made to believe from childhood that saying YES is the key to success and happiness, as it opens new doors. What we are not taught is that saying NO does not necessarily mean losing opportunities. It merely means that after having analyzed a situation to the best of your ability and position, if you feel like saying NO, you say so and follow it up with your actions accordingly. Don't let anyone or anything bully you into saying YES when you are unwilling. Doing something just to please someone is a dangerous form of flattery and should be despised under all circumstances.

"Your mind and heart are agitated because you said YES even though you should have said NO.

"Human tragedy lies in the fact that we build relationships, careers, and situations on a foundation of an unwilling YES. This sham that we create just because we are unable to say NO always starts to misrepresent itself in our lives. So, a relationship that deserves a NO may permanently close the door to another relationship that deserved a YES. A joyless career may actually murder a sparkling talent and so on. If you observe around you, several lives are lived in unhappiness just because they did not have the courage or the guidance to say NO. You owe it to yourself to say NO when it is required.

"Even the three monkeys of the Mahatma were all about practicing the power of saying NO. Saying NO may bring pain temporarily, but the happiness of uncluttering your life will far outweigh any pain."

The Lama was silent after having sermoned his disciple. He looked at the bird, which seemed to acknowledge the receipt of this divine knowledge. And after what looked like a bow of thanks, the bird flew away. *Maybe, this knowledge will help him in his next life.* The Lama smiled.

CHAPTER 5

BUDGE THE GRUDGE

"One good thing about music,
when it hits you, you feel no pain."
—BOB MARLEY

The Billionaire was very particular about his morning routine. He would wake up at 5 a.m. and, after a cold-water bath, sit down to listen to positive affirmations, which his father had recorded for him some 20 years back. It was an invaluable gift. The Billionaire often joked with his friends that his health was probably his worst investment. He did not do yoga or any other physical exercise and was content with mental workouts. He would, holding his cup of chai, mentally visualize the day ahead and plan for it. He was a firm believer in the power of visualizing goals and challenges.

At home, he enjoyed doing mundane work like gardening or making breakfast for his kids in the mornings; he was beginning to understand that this was probably his meditation.

No emails or social media before 8 a.m. was the other rule he followed. He was proud that even in the cold weather of Tibet, he was able to continue with his cold-water showers. He would probably boast about this the next time when he discussed the benefits of a cold-water bath with his wife.

Today, as he sat down to check his email, his face started to burn a deep red. A newspaper in Kazakhstan had just broken the story of corruption in high places and had explicitly named the Billionaire for greasing palms to get the telecom license. The Billionaire was furious. *How could they have the audacity to put the cart before the horse?* Everyone knew that the Billionaire had refused to entertain the authorities, and this was the reason the file was still pending clearance. And now, they were blaming him for something he had not done. Adding to his troubles was the fact that his joint venture with his Singapore investors was now in jeopardy.

News sensationalism to garner higher followership was

prevalent, and the Billionaire had fought this nuisance earlier. It called for retaliation at the highest level. The Billionaire was not used to being pushed around. He knew how to hold grudges and strike back when the time was ripe.

After a lengthy placating call with his investors in Singapore, the Billionaire arrived for his breakfast. Even though it was later than usual, the Monk was waiting for him. Both sat down to have breakfast. The Monk sensed something was simmering inside his partner.

"All good?" Just two words from the Monk were sufficient to open the floodgates of emotions from the Billionaire. The Monk was taken aback by the force of the feelings. He was now at the receiving end of an emotional outburst—unlike yesterday, when he had been the source and the housekeeping staff the receiver. Karma was quick to bite back.

"I am going to sue them, left, right, and center. They don't know whom they have messed with this time," groused the Billionaire. Given the state of emotional affairs, the Monk decided to put off the visit to the Songtsen Monastery, which was scheduled for that day.

This was unfortunate because today was the last day before the Head Lama went into silence. He had agreed to spend personal time with the Billionaire.

The Billionaire decided to spend the rest of the day on video conferences with his legal team and associates. The strategy to strike back was framed, the costs and consequences weighed, and the weapons mobilized, but in his heart, the Billionaire knew the futility of going to war just over a grudge. Ignorance was supposed to be bliss, but the thirst of the ego demon had to be quenched.

It was evening by the time everything was packed up. The Billionaire decided to go for a quiet walk. When he reached the open courtyard, he was surprised to see a bonfire and a group of local artists singing and playing their traditional music on an acoustic guitar. The Monk signaled to him to come and join them. Music was always a mood lifter. As he sat down next to the Monk, his eye caught sight of a young girl. She was a fragile beauty with a charming grace.

Even though the Billionaire did not understand the words, he liked the enthusiasm of the group as they sang and danced around the fire. After a while, the mic found its way to the girl's hand. After a bit of hesitation, the girl stood up and held the mic. The magical spell cast thereafter was unexplainable. Even though the Billionaire did not understand the lyrics, the melancholy in her voice was heart-wrenching. The audience was drugged with emotion.

It was probably the same kind of spell which the legendary Lata Mangeshkar must have cast when she blessed Indians by singing the classic "Ae Mere Watan Ke Logo" for the first time. The song ended, but no one moved. Probably someone had to snap them back to reality. Gradually, people returned from the magical world. But one thing was sure: Everyone who heard the song that night knew they had experienced something divine. Something more than a song.

"So, what did the girl sing about?" asked the Billionaire, after absorbing the melancholic voice.

"Giving up on grudges," replied the Monk, who was also equally under the spell of the song. "It's an old folk tale about how an idyllic village was torn apart because of a small misunderstanding, how war ravaged the town and left behind a trail of despair and destruction. All because we as humans like to carry grudges. We can call it what we want—ego, vengeance, honor, or envy—nomenclature aside, it all stands for that desire to strike back at someone who may or may not have harmed you, but you undoubtedly think that harm was caused and hence harbor the need for retribution.

"The people of the village spent valuable resources like time, money, and sometimes even relationships only to be seen as winners. Most ended up as losers instead.

"The problem with a grudge is that it is a double-edged sword," continued the Monk, now moving beyond the interpretation of the song. "It has the potential to cut both ways, and at times, the action born out of a grudge harms you more than it harms the target. Tragically, quite a few grudges are a result of a misunderstanding, miscommunication, and selective understanding; in reality, they could be buried quickly."

The Billionaire became uncomfortable on hearing the story and the Monk's add-in. He had just spent his entire day planning retribution, and here was a story of revenge that backfired for everyone involved. Was the staging of the song a deliberate effort by the Monk to convey a message, or had a higher power designed the evening for him to learn the futility of nursing a grudge?

"So, what should one do if he has been wronged?" asked the Billionaire with sincerity in his voice.

The Monk looked at the embers that were still shimmering and waging a losing battle with the cold breeze. He reflected on how the hot day had changed into a cold night. Tibet was probably one of few geographical wonders where in a single day one could experience the extreme temperature of both +35 degrees and -17 degrees, all within 24 hours.

After reflecting on the question, the Monk spoke with authority.

"Learn to forgive and forget. Sacrificing present happiness to settle a score of the past in the future is not worth it. Life is too short for carrying grudges. Newspapers are full of these tragic stories in which people and families destroy their lives and are living just to pursue a grudge. One must always remember that forgiving is not a weakness.

"But at the same time, one must be bold enough to clarify and seek an explanation of another's hurtful actions. Don't believe in gossip; speak your heart to the person. You will be surprised how dialog can resolve the most challenging stand-offs. Don't indulge, encourage, or generate gossip. Your life is more valuable than just being a postbox.

"Also, one must learn to say sorry. No harm has ever come from being wrong and acknowledging it. There is no shame in apologizing if it can settle matters. Dialog and arbitration are far more effective and efficient than litigation. The money, time, and anxiety spent on litigation mostly offset any gains that may occur.

"And lastly, develop a sense of humor. Sometimes, ignoring or laughing off someone's hurtful comments can save you a lot of heartburn. The truth is several people do not mean what they say, or maybe they are speaking under influence and do not intend any harm. If you start taking everything people say seriously, it will be a tough life to live. Learn to ignore."

The Monk did have some aces up his sleeve on worldly matters! The Billionaire enacted a hats-off gesture to acknowledge the depth of the Monk's wisdom. The courts in Kazakhstan could do with one less piece of litigation.

CHAPTER 6

HEALTHY BODY, HAPPY BODY

"I heard a definition once: Happiness is
health and a short memory! I wish I'd invented it
because it is very true."

—AUDREY HEPBURN

It had been 15 days in Shangri-La, and the Billionaire had settled in well. Since there was Wi-Fi and a working desk in his suite, he was able to run his empire from the comfort of his room. The body had also begun to respond positively to the pure air, the simple food, and the regular long walks. *My body was starting to age in reverse*, thought the Billionaire.

Being a Tuesday evening, the hotel was quiet. Fewer guests and the weekly staff holiday resulted in a deserted lobby area. The Billionaire and the Monk sat idling their time, like two college kids talking about nothing. It was like the carefree salad days of youth.

"You know, you are looking much fitter now, partner," remarked the Monk.

"I know! Just this morning, I noticed a reduction in my waistline. My back pain is also better now. I am hoping to be able to get back on my Enfield bike from my college days, once I am back home," said the Billionaire jokingly.

"You know health is given a lot of attention in our monastic life," a soft voice joined the conversation. The Chief Lama had come to check on his students who were running the thangka painting classes for guests on the property and had noticed the partners enjoying lounging for once and decided to join them.

Sometimes there is divine energy in doing nothing.

"We Buddhists consider this body to be a loan to us, and it is our responsibility to keep it healthy for the soul to reside in. It goes without doubt that a healthy body can be a crucial ingredient in the happiness cocktail of life," the Lama spoke gently, as he settled on the empty chair next to the fireplace.

"You will recall, on a day that your body is sick, your spirit feels low and the heart depressed. This simple experience is sufficient to acknowledge that being unhealthy makes being happy difficult. It is, therefore, necessary to acknowledge and appreciate the value of a healthy body to your happiness quotient and treat the body accordingly."

The Chief Lama was making sense. A healthy body did make one happy.

"We believe a healthy body is a result of three fundamental aspects: nutrition, exercise, and rest. All three elements play a vital role in maintaining and enhancing your health. No single component is sufficient, and all three aspects should be balanced for a fit and happy body.

"You must have heard of the American nutritionist Victor Lindlahr, who in the 1920s gave the Western world the phrase 'you are what you eat.' It means that the food you eat defines both your physical and mental well-being. We in Tibet have been practicing this for ages.

"This phrase is more relevant in this era because we are surrounded by choices in food that were probably never available to humankind ever before. For the first time in human history, our civilization eats for the pleasure of a meal rather than for the needs of the body. Unlike our ancestors, who probably hunted for lunch, we merely open a packet, and hey, presto, lunch is served!

"However, eating is not the same as nourishing the body. The human body has its well-defined requirements that are needed for a healthy life. Depriving the body of nutrition can have serious side effects. Once you begin to eat well, you will see it manifest positively both in your emotional happiness and physical well-being.

"*The second aspect of a healthy body is physical exercise.* Nowadays, people lead a sedentary lifestyle. Easy access to both machines and equipment has reduced a lot of physical load from our daily lives. Even monks have started to drive around in SUVs!" The Lama took another shot at the Monk with a mischievous smile. "While this has permitted and enhanced our ability to pursue mental work, the body still needs its share of physical activity. Various scientific studies have shown that there is a strong correlation between physical exercise and happiness. It is scientifically proven that exercise increases endorphins and other feel-good brain chemicals. It also reduces levels of stress hormones called cortisol. Even small amounts of physical exercise can have significant healing effects on mental illness like depression, anxiety, stress, and other emotional problems—even 10–15 minutes of structured exercise like yoga or a long walk is a good start.

"*Finally, good sleep is important for the body.* Our highest teachers are often heard as saying 'Sleep is the best meditation.'" The Lama closed his eyes in reverence, thinking of His Holiness. Since taking the name of the Dalai Lama could cause trouble, the Lama did not name the speaker of those golden words, but everyone was aware of the Dalai Lama's love for sleep.

"Our sleep has a direct bearing upon both our physical and mental health. Rest is an essential aspect of defining our physical and psychological well-being. It is nature's way of repairing our physical structure. Insufficient sleep has been linked to various lifestyle diseases like diabetes, obesity, heart diseases, reduced immunity, and reduced life expectancy. Sleep deprivation is quickly becoming a silent public health crisis. The idea of ignoring sleep to chase our daydreams is now getting dangerous."

The scientific precision with which the Lama spoke would have held up in any medical conference.

"Any tips for good sleep, Guruji?" asked the Billionaire.

"Unless you have reached the stage which requires medical intervention, in which case you should consult a doctor, the tricks to a sound sleep are quite simple. I am sure your partner knows lots of them. He is probably a PhD on the subject," joked the Lama. The Monk smiled.

"The ones I practice are quite simple:

- Have a regular sleep-wake schedule.
- Sleep when you're exhausted, to avoid tossing and turning.

- Before bedtime, engage in mindfulness through exercises like knitting, painting, or reading.
- Avoid chemical foods and drinks which contain caffeine, alcohol, and nicotine.
- Make your bedroom a comfortable sleep environment.
- Avoid thinking of issues that give rise to anxiety.
- Avoid looking at your phone screen just before sleeping.

"In general, the idea is to help your body relax and maintain the body clock to facilitate sound sleep."

After a brief pause, the Lama got up from his seat, adjusted the firewood, and, looking at the Billionaire, concluded the discussion with a comment which struck a chord with the Billionaire.

"Lastly, always remember that no one can adopt your body pain and disease. Medical advancement and money can only subdue your illness and pain; it can prolong your life, but the agony of illness and its unhappiness is yours. Family and friends can sympathize, provide moral support, and emotional assurance, but none of them can replace your body with their healthy body. Fighting an illness is always a lone and unhappy battle."

Even though the words had been spoken in the signature soft tone by the Lama, the silence of the reception area had made them loud enough even for the girl on reception duty to grasp and understand. Another unexpected soul had benefited from the Lama's wisdom.

From that day onwards, the Billionaire added 30 minutes of physical exercise to his morning routine and vowed to follow the sleep rituals.

CHAPTER 7

BUYING HAPPINESS

"When I was young I thought that money
was the most important thing in life; now that
I am old I know that it is."

—OSCAR WILDE

There was an unusual excitement in the reception hall in the afternoon. A group of business school students from Shanghai had just arrived. The Monk was an active member of the local industry body and very active in promoting entrepreneurial skills among the local population. From beekeeping to tea marketing, he would often roam the country, giving presentations on the positive effects of social enterprises on the lives of village populations. As a result, every year, four to five groups from prestigious Chinese business schools would come to Shangri-La to experience firsthand the working of meaningful social enterprises. This was one of those groups.

The Monk enthusiastically approached the Billionaire with an idea.

"Why don't you give a small talk on money today? The students all understand English, and I am sure they will be thrilled to meet and hear from a billionaire."

The idea appealed to the Billionaire; cross-culture interactions always brought a new perspective to his learning, and his mind began making preparations for the evening. The question was how to make the talk interesting for students. So, the Billionaire titled the session "Yes, You Can Buy Happiness," knowing very well that the contrarian view would find appeal with the young audience.

The informal get-together in the dining hall began with the Monk introducing the Billionaire and his achievements. A loud round of applause welcomed the Billionaire as he was handed the mic.

"*Tashi delek*, everyone. I welcome you to our hotel and hope you have a great stay," the Billionaire began.

"We all have heard the saying 'money cannot buy happiness.' What if I tell you that this is a lie? What if I tell you that money is among the essential components of happiness?

It may be contrary to what you have been taught, but it is the truth."

The audience was all ears.

"Let me explain. Both money and happiness are much bigger and wider concepts than what most people understand. Happiness is not indulgence, and money is not merely possessing cash."

The Billionaire paused so that the audience would be able to grasp what he just said.

"It is important to distinguish between money as a concept and the reckless pursuit of money as an action. The latter is certainly not desirable, but the former is essential. Money is an integral part of our happiness quotient. It is one of the many other components that make a person happy. It is an important asset to have. But is it the only component? *No*."

Sounds of approval were beginning to come from the audience.

"In fact, money as a concept is made up of four dimensions. Once you learn about these four dimensions, you will realize that money is a much bigger concept than commonly understood and the link between happiness and money is inevitable.

"When I started my career, I used to believe that there

were two dimensions of money—*earning* and *consumption*. As a result, I always failed to get happiness from whatever big or small amount of money I had. However, as the hair on my head started to turn gray, I began to learn about the other two dimensions of money. And ever since I began syncing all the four dimensions, life has been full of happiness bought by money!

"Today, I am going to share these two ignored aspects with you."

The excitement among the audience was palpable now. The thought of unexpectedly receiving money secrets from a billionaire was pulsating through the crowd.

The Billionaire continued, after a sip of water: "The four dimensions of money are

1. Income
2. Savings
3. Investments
4. Consumption

"Income, salary, dividend, profit, interest, fee, or compensation all refer to the same thing. It is the reward for our efforts paid in cash or kind. It is the most visible and instant element of money that we all understand.

"*We work, we earn*. Simple equation.

"However, income alone is not money. Income is only one of the four pillars of money. The moment we start equating income with money, we lose track. This is the reason you hear several people complain that no matter how much they earn, they can never be happy. The truth is they have no understanding that income is not money. They may be generating cash flow, but are not making money. Income is what you earn. It is one of the dimensions of money, and money itself is just one component of happiness. How can one hope to get happiness only because he has an income?

"This knowledge is the first differentiating factor between happiness and sadness from money.

"Now, moving to the second dimension of money, consumption. This is a well-practiced use of income. Some of us live for this; others die of this!" A small burst of laughter erupted in the room.

"Most of us look at the consumption of income as the source of happiness from money. If we can buy what we want, we assume that we will be happy. However, when consumption of income fails to make us happy, we quickly say that money cannot buy happiness. This is the second time we make the same mistake, that is, using one dimension to define happiness." The crowd was beginning to understand the thought process and nodded in agreement.

"Ironically, even though income and consumption alone

cannot add much to our overall happiness, the reckless pursuit of income and mindless consumption can become the biggest reasons for unhappiness. So, in effect, they may add less to happiness, but if abused, they take away happiness disproportionately. Yes, it is a strange relationship, and you must take a pause and understand and analyze the relationship."

The audience was silent. They were probably taking in the big ideas. The Monk sat in the corner, smiling. He knew what the kids were learning here in these few minutes was more than what they would learn in their entire two years at college.

"Now let's talk about the two secret but critical dimensions of money and how they shape your happiness. These two dimensions are the real source of happiness from money, so listen carefully," commanded the Billionaire, who had by now transformed into the business tycoon that he was and demanded, and received, rapt attention from his audience.

"The young think savings are for the elderly. The elderly regret not having thought of it in their youth! Since savings are a voluntary use of money, several people choose to ignore it. Savings is the third dimension of money. Most of us fail to visualize the utility of savings, till we reach the stage when we need the savings. So, it's that dimension of money that we don't see till we need it. And as they say, *if you have not planned for it on a sunny day, you aren't going to get it on a rainy day.*

"Everyone should have a plan and strict discipline to save money. One must remember that savings are different from investments, something which we will cover later. It is, therefore, always good to check your savings against the following parameters.

1. Liquidity—Savings should be highly liquid, that is, you should be able to get the money in your hands quickly and with the least cost.
2. Accessibility—Savings should be accessible in all geographical locations and at all times.
3. Risk-free—Savings should be risk-free and not subject to any market terms and conditions.

"Only when your savings tick all the above boxes can you call them savings and be relaxed and happy."

The Billionaire was surprised to see that the Chief Lama was also among the audience. He smiled at the Chief Lama, acknowledging his presence.

"Lastly, the glamorous component of money, from which legends are made—investments."

The Billionaire had made his money with investments

that had been global game-changers. From high-tech disruptors to traditional value picks, his reputation as an investor was remarkable. It was whispered in the business community that his ability as an individual to generate returns was on par with some of the most exceptional hedge fund teams globally.

"In simple words, investment is making your money work as hard as you do," continued the Billionaire.

"In finance, the concept of the time value of money explains to us that over time money loses its value due to inflation. In simple terms, 100 dollars today is less valuable than 100 dollars 20 years ago. This is why, when you sit with the elders of your family, they speak with much fondness how they could buy the world in their time at the price of a biscuit pack today. Exaggerated tales, but the idea holds. Over time, money loses its value. It is, therefore, important that you make your money work and grow so that it keeps pace with the value erosion.

"I will try and give you some rules on investments. Understand the concepts behind them and then use them in the real world. You may want to note them down."

Some people fidgeted to get pen and paper; others simply started to record the Billionaire on their phones. *Generation Z*, thought the Billionaire.

"Rule #1: Risk-Reward: This is the golden rule of

all investments. Higher the risk, higher the return. Every investment option offers a return that matches its risk profile. If anyone says that the investment is as safe as a bank deposit but it provides a higher return, it is a lie.

"Higher the risk, higher the possibility of capital (money invested) loss. Understand your risk profile based on your age, personal requirements, family requirements, and income stream. Most people tend to behave like Mel Gibson in *Braveheart* and overestimate their risk capacity. Be honest about your risk profile and avoid any investments that do not match your risk profile. Diversification across asset classes helps spread risk. However, lower risk will mean a lower return.

"Rule #2: Return of capital (money invested) is more important than return on capital (income).

"Rule #3: Don't ape others' investments just because they appear to be doing better than you. Remember, everyone has a different risk profile and financial goals. Investing is a long-term process. Compounding wealth is the main agenda of investment, and it can only be achieved by being disciplined, systematic, and persistent over time.

"Rule #4: If you don't know, always entrust your money with experts who have proven themselves over different market cycles and situations. And remember, there are no free lunches. Anyone trying to sell you an investment idea for free is indeed hiding something. Be aware of all vested interests.

"Rule #5: Never take a loan for an unproductive or depreciating asset.

"Rule #6: Always remember as you start your economic life that it is not the cost of living that is expensive but the cost of lifestyle that is expensive. A good rule is to allocate the least to consumption and most to investments. Moreover, savings should be sufficient for six months of living expenses at any point in time. Build a savings corpus before investing.

"Rule #7: Learn to control the temptation to consume. Minimalism is a secret source of wealth creation.

"And, lastly, my favorite one, which I always share with people who are married or are going to get married— Jewelry is not an investment; it is consumption." The Billionaire ended the talk with a bow.

The audience was on their feet, clapping and cheering. They realized the importance of the evening and surrounded the Billionaire for a selfie marathon.

The next morning, pinned to the Billionaire's hotel room door was a note:

I think after understanding money as explained by you, I agree that money can buy happiness if you know where to shop! The truth is that now I know that having money may or may not give you happiness, but not having money will certainly not give you happiness.

You have shown us that we live in a world where money is an essential tool to shape our happiness. The critical thing to remember is that it is not the only tool.

Thank You
Chief Lama

CHAPTER 8

Homecoming: The Monk's Story

"In human relationships, kindness and
lies are worth a thousand truths."

—GRAHAM GREENE

In the year 1993, a group of Tibetan refugees living in
McLeodganj in India decided to return to their homeland.
They did not hold anything against the Government of
India and carried His Holiness the Dalai Lama in godlike
respect, but they were simply tired of living a stateless life.
With the blessings of His Holiness the Dalai Lama, they
chose to take control of their own lives, and they decided
it was time to return and rebuild their lives in the land of
their ancestors. The Khampa warriors, the clan to which
the Monk belonged, had come with His Holiness as his

official army in 1959. It had a glorious past, but now only memories remained.

The Monk, who had a bright future in the monastic hierarchy in McLeodganj, bid farewell to his teacher and quit his monkhood. In his heart, he knew he was never meant to be a monk. This was his opportunity. He joined his *pala* (father) as the Khampa warriors retreated to restart their lives in their ancient land, Tibet.

Surprisingly, the Government of China welcomed them back with open arms. They were granted lands and government jobs. To the Government of China, they were its citizens who had returned home. However, the journey back to their villages was full of physical and mental challenges, and it took a toll on the caravan. They had chosen to trek along the ancient tea trade route, which started in present-day Myanmar, continued via Kolkata, and went all the way into Tibet, terminating at Pu'er in the Yunnan Province of present-day China. The ancient tea route was a testimony of the grit and entrepreneurial spirit of the Tibetan people and was full of stories and folklore.

During their 53-day trek to their village of Gyalthang (Tibetan for Zhongdian), the Monk, still in his early 20s, and his *pala* nourished their father and son bond for the first time. Since the Monk had been admitted to a monastery at the age of four, he hardly knew his father. This tedious journey was his comfort time with his *pala*. They talked about the past, planned for the future, displayed their strengths, and exposed their fears. They shared their stories and understandings of life. These were beautiful days in an ugly situation, and the father and son enjoyed each other's companionship. Probably, it was God's way of compensating for the fact that Pala would leave for his heavenly abode on the 17th day of returning to their ancestral home.

The Monk, who had lost his mother at childbirth, suddenly found himself orphaned in a land that was his, yet he was a stranger there. Having just reentered the realms of worldly life had its own set of challenges.

The words of the Buddha were to be his guide now: "Believe nothing because a wise man said it. Believe nothing because it is generally held. Believe nothing because it is written. Believe nothing because it is said to be divine. Believe only what you yourself judge to be true."

One forte that the Monk developed as he went about molding his life was his ability to build relationships and maintain them. He had a natural knack for solving relationship problems. Listening, understanding, negotiating, and empathizing came naturally to him. His skill of asking the right questions and communicating his needs and his sense of humor always paved the way for him.

The Monk realized that relationships were the bedrock of

happiness in life. Since humans are social animals, we move around in a circle of relationships, some that we inherit and others that we develop. How we handle relationships has a direct bearing on our happiness quotient. Broken relationships can be a heavy burden on your happiness. Sour relationships are among the biggest reasons for unhappiness in our life.

He also observed that relationships are complex as they are a result of two minds and hearts trying to interact with each other. Body language, verbal communication, digital communication, geographical limitations, actions, non-actions, external events, physical situations, and many more controllable and non-controllable elements influence and define any relationship. However, after years of practice, he had understood the one trick that had the power to make all relationships an eternal source of happiness in life.

This was the key the Monk had discovered: The easiest way to handle a relationship is to step into the shoes of the other person.

The Monk realized that with this little imaginative effort, relationships become so much more joyous and satisfying. Be it your relationship with your spouse, or with your parents, or your children, or your office colleagues, by merely looking at the situation from the other person's viewpoint and understanding their perspective, one can master the art of happy relationships.

Most of us are too full of ourselves and fail to give the other person's perspective any value. But in doing so, we sometimes throw away the most precious people in our lives only to embrace unhappiness—another human tragedy.

In a world that was falling apart because of failed relationships, the Monk had found his niche. He quickly began to apply this knowledge and gained a reputation as an excellent negotiator. His success at resolving both minor and major conflicts, negotiating win-win solutions, and his good-boy charm brought him to the knowledge of the government authorities. The government quickly lapped up the opportunity to project him as the face of a progressive Tibet. This opened new doors for the Monk, and he was appointed to various forums and committees to represent Tibet. It was these turns of events that led the Monk to join the trade delegation sent to Kathmandu to promote the tourism potential of the town of Shangri-La. That's where he met the Billionaire and a new life as a partner to a billionaire began.

The Monk was staring at his meditation mandala. But his thoughts were focused on the events of the last few weeks. *Fascinating past few weeks. Just when you feel that you have seen*

it all and learned it all, the Divine sends you a new syllabus. Novel though. The new perspectives on happiness that both Guruji and the Billionaire have shared over the last few weeks have significantly added to my knowledge chest on happiness.

Recalling his commitment to sharing his list of "Happiness Hacks" with the Billionaire, the Monk quickly drew out his diary and began to copy the notes on a piece of paper. The Monk loved the Americans for their slang dictionary.

CHAPTER 9

CHOOSING THE PATH:
THE BILLIONAIRE'S STORY

"Two roads diverged in a wood and I took the one less traveled by, and that has made all the difference."

—ROBERT FROST

The Billionaire's father was an industrialist in his own right. Lovingly called Seth Babu by all, he was an uncomplicated man. Hard work, family time, and service to God were his prime pursuits in life. They lived a very comfortable life in a mansion and had a fleet of cars and an army of servants in spotless livery. This was the India of a socialist era with the license raj, but Seth Babu knew how to expand his commercial interests. Seth Babu was a well-connected man and always managed to pull the right strings. In the year 1988, when the Billionaire decided to drop out of college just 15 days after joining it, his father was not angry. He merely asked the Billionaire what the plan was, half-expecting the Billionaire to say that he would like to live off his inheritance. Seth Babu was pleasantly surprised when the Billionaire told him that he wanted to go to Bombay and start working at the stock exchange. The Billionaire also got his father to promise that Seth Babu would not pull any strings to advance the Billionaire's career. Seth Babu was happy. A "self-made man" was the ultimate title any man could have in his life. His son had chosen his path.

The night before the departure to Bombay, Seth Babu called the Billionaire to his study and gave him the only wisdom that the Billionaire had ever borrowed from anyone.

"Among the most challenging aspects of life is to learn to align career goals with happiness. Sacrificing happiness for career enhancement is not okay. Similarly, being happy without a worthy career is unacceptable," spoke Seth Babu in a dispassionate tone. Displaying emotions in the study was a strict no-no for Seth Babu.

"The moment you realize that work is more than just a source of income, your perspective toward work and life will change. As hackneyed as it may sound, most of us enter into a career either because our parents want us to or because we think that we can lead a comfortable monetary life. Fortunately, you have chosen to avoid this trap. By the time we realize that we may have chosen the wrong life, we are either under the EMI burden or simply too afraid to bring about a change in life. So, we maintain the status quo and glide along, always planning an exit but never pressing the evacuation button. This does not end well, and we go down with the aircraft, so to speak!"

Seth Babu loved the use of aviation metaphors. Even at this age and social standing, Seth Babu actively pursued his hobby of model airplanes. In fact, in all job interviews that he presided over, the most important question was always regarding the candidate's hobby. Seth Babu felt that if a man did not pursue a hobby, it was a character flaw!

"The truth is there are successful and rich people from all walks of life. Individuals who have the confidence and ability to embrace happiness have found money and fame in the most socially different careers. Poets, writers, painters, architects, actors, and athletes all have the same opportunities to make money and reputation as any conventional career. The important thing is to be the best in your field of work. The world does not value mediocrity in any field but rewards meritocracy in every field," continued Seth Babu.

"People who chose to work for their heart and persist until they reached the pinnacle of excellence in their discipline always leave a mark on society and their era. Money is a by-product; the happiness of excellence is their true goal. Remember, son, now that you have chosen to be an investor, be the best." The last words still ring in the Billionaire's ears when he is making the final sign-off on any investment deal.

Once in Bombay, the Billionaire had taken to the world of Dalal Street as the proverbial fish takes to water. Starting as a jobber for a Parsi broker to becoming the Big Bull and dealmaker of the Indian stock exchange in 32 years was a storybook in itself. All through this period, the Billionaire never forgot the evening in Seth Babu's office. Thereafter, Seth Babu Incorporated and the Billionaire had made money hand over fist working together. Seth Babu's instinct and the Billionaire's tenacity made a formidable hunting duo in the corporate arena.

Tomorrow, at this time, he would be back in his world, but the lessons learned in Shangri-La over the past 20 days would shape his happiness for the rest of his life. He mused, *Was it not Lenin who said, "There are decades where nothing happens, and there are weeks where decades happen"?*

The Billionaire also felt it was essential that his children, and their children in time, inherit this knowledge of happiness just like he inherited the lesson of life from his father.

With this thought, the Billionaire began writing his notes, as agreed between him and the Monk on the first day.

CHAPTER 10

FAREWELL

"Friendship is always a sweet responsibility,
never an opportunity."

—KAHLIL GIBRAN

The Monk idolized Mithun Chakraborty, Bappi Da, and Bollywood. The India of the 80s was where his youth had taken shape, and like all love stories of adolescences, his love for Bollywood always remained close to his heart. "I Am a Disco Dancer" was the one song that always welcomed you into his car; it was the first song on all his playlists.

As they drove to the airport, the Billionaire and the Monk discussed the final commercial aspects and prospects of the hotel. The Billionaire approved of the quality and business management standards at the hotel and even suggested doing another property in Lhasa. The Monk promised he would study opportunities and share them with the team.

Both knew that once on the plane, the Billionaire would be lost in his loop of work, and thinking about a small project in Tibet would be the last priority. But both played along.

It was only when they hit the expressway leading up to the airport terminal, the last leg of the journey, that both fell silent. "Zihaal-e-Miskeen Mukon Ba-Ranjush" from the film *Ghulami* played in the background. The Billionaire had never understood the meaning of the Urdu words in the song. Still, like that evening at the hotel, the melancholy of Lata Mangeshkar's voice in this song always captivated him.

The Monk understood the song. He once practically begged a *maulvi* to explain to him the meaning of those words by the medieval poet Amir Khusrau, adapted brilliantly by Gulzar:

Zihaal-e-Miskeen Mukon Ba-Ranjish, Bahaal-e-Hijra
  Bechara Dil Hai
Don't look at my poor heart with enmity,
it's still fresh from the wounds of separation.

They realized that even for their mature and adult life, the past few weeks had been extraordinary and never again in their lives would they be able to relive these days of introspection and self-discovery.

As the luggage was being unloaded from the trunk of the car, the Monk took out a neatly folded sheet of paper and handed it to the Billionaire. The Billionaire smiled and gave him a similar piece of paper. The Monk was not expecting the Billionaire to have bothered about writing the lessons, but the humility of the man was what defined him.

A tear fell to say thank you.

It was time to say goodbye, partner!

EPILOGUE

"This too shall pass."

—OLD PERSIAN ADAGE

Are you happy?—The question that started the quest.

Both the Billionaire and the Monk saw happiness as an isolated object. One had money, the other had knowledge, but unfortunately, happiness eluded both of them. However, once they started learning from each other and their surroundings, they discovered that the secret to happiness lay in understanding and realizing that *happiness is attained and not achieved.*

Both found that happiness is not a quantifiable goal that can be achieved, but instead, it is a qualitative state of living that has to be attained.

They learned that though a dictionary may define the word "happiness," there is no one definition of happiness.

Every age, society, religion, philosopher, guru, or individual has a different understanding of what happiness is.

*So, **what** is happiness?*

In the story, the Billionaire and the Monk learn that happiness is harmony between the mind and heart. It is a balance between ambition and laughter. Happiness is not about sacrificing or acquiring. They appreciate the fact that happiness is the pursuit of money via the route of minimalism; however, happiness is not a destination at the same time. They acknowledge that happiness is the courage of saying NO yet keeping alive one's curiosity and creativity by saying YES and exploring. They uncover the wisdom that happiness lies in respecting both "sorry" and "thank you" and realize that happiness is dependent on everyone yet independent of anyone.

Finally, they discover that happiness is not as complicated a concept as it is projected to be and that happiness is nothing but the sum of the ordinary elements of daily life, done well and with gratitude.

Now, when they are asked "Are you happy?" both truly understand the question and know the answer.

Knowledge Points

"Happiness is when what you think, what you say, and what you do are in harmony."

—MAHATMA GANDHI

THE BILLIONAIRE'S NOTES

1. Minimalism helps you unclutter both mental and physical space.

2. An uncluttered mind leads to focus, consistency, and discipline in life.

3. Anything that helps you connect with your inner self is meditation.

4. Living in harmony with nature is, in itself, a source of happiness.

5. Nurturing grudges is fertile soil for the weeds of unhappiness to grow.

6. Being wise yet ignorant is essential for happiness.

7. No one can share your disease or body pain.

8. Ambition, passion, and hard work multiply happiness in life.

9. A sense of humor is a valuable happiness magnet.

THE MONK'S HAPPINESS LEARNINGS

1. Well-defined goals are a must for happiness.

2. Maintaining a to-do list increases productivity and builds confidence.

3. Technology is a tool and should not be allowed to become the master.

4. Being grateful for what you have is more important than blaming others for what you don't have.

5. Blaming multiplies the negativity of defeat.

6. Learning to say NO is essential for being happy.

7. Money = Income + Savings + Investments + Consumption.

8. Relationships that are based on respect attract happiness.

9. Asking is the key to receiving.

Letter from the Author

Dear Reader,

Thank you for giving your valuable time for reading this simple story. I hope that the story has brought you closer to the goal that you were seeking when you chose to begin to read this book. Humankind's quest for happiness is eternal, and I hope that I have added value to your life by sharing my perspective about happiness.

This book has been in the making for years. I have been fortunate to observe life through many different roles, situations, and perspectives. As they say, the good, the bad, and the ugly are all lessons that experience taught me.

Somewhere on this journey, I realized that the beauty of life lies in the contradictions it offers. Often the right decisions yield the wrong consequences and vice versa. The most significant defeats turn into the greatest victories at the last moment, and even though it is the sun that causes the rainbow, the credit goes to the rain! It is, therefore, essential to always be grateful for whatever life gives and maintain a sense of humor even in the most tiring times because life has a mind of its own, which is beyond our realm of control. No matter how towering a challenge may seem, human perseverance will always outgrow it.

The Billionaire and the Monk live within us— the mind and the heart. Every day, we are faced with the dilemma of balancing the voice of the mind with the call of the heart. The mind sees and the heart feels, and it is the harmony between them that gives us happiness. Happiness lies in the balance.

I hope the lessons shared in this story help you attain this harmony and happiness. *It is crucial to remember that, no matter what has been the past or where you stand today, you can always begin fresh—the future depends on today. Every tomorrow starts today.*

Lastly, if this book has helped you in your quest for happiness, do share its knowledge with others. We need to help others see the beauty of life beyond the drudgery of our daily struggles and help them learn that the first step to a happy world is a happy self.

I would love to hear your views on the book.

You can email me at ask@vibhorkumarsingh.com and share your views on the story. You can also visit our website www.vibhorkumarsingh.com for more details.

Thanking you, with best regards,

Vibhor Kumar Singh

Acknowledgments

It is only when you sit down to write a book that you realize a book is a project that requires much more than just creative capabilities. My path from idea to publication has been long and winding, but it has been made memorable and enjoyable by all the people who supported me, inspired me, and encouraged me.

I am thankful to my mother, Kunwarani Meena Singh, for her guidance, blessings, and continuous encouragement to strive for excellence in all spheres of life.

I am thankful to Rahul Chaudhary, Neil Pickering, Anil Nayar, and Dr. (Mrs.) Ridha Singh Gupta for being the first readers of the text and giving their valuable inputs.

I am thankful to my wife, Shakuntala, for continually supporting all my endeavors and coping with my work-life imbalance!

I am thankful to my son, Ayushraj, for his valuable inputs on the content and styling. He was my go-to guy for bouncing off ideas during the project.

I am thankful to my daughter, Aaradhya, for bringing all the smiles and laughter.

I would like to thank Dr. Binod Chaudhary, Pankaj Dubey, Kelden Dakpa, Rakesh Mathur, S. D. Dhakal, Dr. Abhijeet Darak, Dr. Anant Gupta, Dr. Raj Ratna Darak, and all my mentors, friends, and family members who have been a source of inspiration and happiness over the years. Each one of them, in their unique way, has shaped my thought process and influenced this book.

I would like to thank the team at Grand Central Publishing for helping put the U.S. publication process together.

Lastly, I would like to thank the Almighty upstairs, who I firmly believe loves me, for having made life a challenging yet pleasant journey and giving me the opportunity and strength to pursue a fulfilling and meaningful life.

ABOUT THE AUTHOR

Vibhor Kumar Singh grew up in the Indian Himalayas and attended the London School of Economics and Political Science. He is a stock market professional, and he lives with his wife, mother, and two children in Noida, in northern India. He loves chai, history, and Bollywood films. This is his first book.